For Peter and Ella

Cats Sleep Anywhere was designed and produced by Frances Lincoln Limited,
4 Torriano Mews, Torriano Avenue, London NW5 2RZ, England

Cats Sleep Anywhere
Copyright © 1996 by Frances Lincoln Ltd.
Text copyright © 1957 by Gervase Farjeon
Illustrations copyright © 1996 by Anne Mortimer
Printed in Hong Kong. All rights reserved.

Library of Congress Cataloging-in-Publication Data
Farjeon, Eleanor, 1881–1965.
  Cats sleep anywhere : [poem] / by Eleanor Farjeon ; illustrated by Anne
Mortimer.
    p.   cm.
  Summary: Cats sleep on tables, chairs, sofas, in closets, in shoeboxes—all
around the house.
  ISBN 0-06-027334-8. — ISBN 0-06-027335-6 (lib. bdg.)
  1. Cats—Juvenile poetry.   2. Children's poetry, English.   [1. Cats—Poetry.
2. English poetry.]   I. Mortimer, Anne, ill.   II. Title.
PR6011.A67C35   1996   95-50371
821'.912—dc20   CIP
                                                          AC

1 2 3 4 5 6 7 8 9 10
❖
First Edition

Cats Sleep Anywhere

Eleanor Farjeon

illustrated by

Anne Mortimer

HarperCollinsPublishers

Cats sleep anywhere,

Any table,

Any chair,

Top of piano,

Window-ledge,

In the middle,

On the edge,

Open drawer,

Empty shoe,

Anybody's lap will do,

Fitted in a cardboard box,

In the cupboard

With your frocks—

Anywhere!

They don't care!

Cats sleep

Anywhere.